PRESENTED TO:

_____

FROM:

_____

DATE:

_____

Tommy Nelson, PO Box 141000, Nashville, TN 37214

Published in Nashville, Tennessee, by Tommy Nelson. Tommy Nelson is an imprint of Thomas Nelson. Thomas Nelson is a registered trademark of HarperCollins Christian Publishing, Inc.

Tommy Nelson titles may be purchased in bulk for educational, business, fundraising, or sales promotional use. For information, please e-mail SpecialMarkets@ThomasNelson.com.

Written by Jean Fischer

Illustrated by Katie Rewse

Library of Congress Cataloging-in-Publication Data

Names: Galvan, Jose, 1987- author. | Galvan, Liz Marie, author. | Rewse, Katie, illustrator.
Title: We belong to each other / Jose Galvan and Liz Marie Galvan ; illustrated by Katie Rewse.
Description: Nashville, Tennessee : Thomas Nelson, 2021. | Audience: Ages 4-8 | Summary: A lamb named Grace searches longingly for a family until she finds others like her at White Cottage Farm.
Identifiers: LCCN 2020029790 | ISBN 9781400224746 (hardcover)
Subjects: CYAC: Belonging (Social psychology)--Fiction. | Identity--Fiction. | Family life--Fiction. | Christian life--Fiction.
Classification: LCC PZ7.1.G349 We 2021 | DDC [E]--dc23
LC record available at https://lccn.loc.gov/2020029790

Printed in Korea

21 22 23 24 25 SAM 10 9 8 7 6 5 4 3 2 1

Mfr: SAM / Seoul, Korea / February 2021 / PO #9589879

To our son,
Copeland Beau—You are our
true rainbow after a dark storm of
longing to grow our family. We love you to the
moon and back. We truly belong to each other.

And to Cope's amazing birth mom—We know that
our words will never be enough to show our gratitude,
but we are so thankful for your selfless and courageous
decision to choose us to be Cope's parents.

WE BELONG TO EACH OTHER

JOSE GALVAN AND LIZ MARIE GALVAN

ILLUSTRATED BY KATIE REWSE

Tommy NELSON®

An Imprint of Thomas Nelson

Rumble, rumble, rumble.
Down a bumpy road, a truck drove
home with a precious load.

Baby Grace prayed, "Wherever
I'm going, wherever I'll be, please,
God, let there be sheep like me."

The smiling lady said, "Welcome home, Grace!"

The kind man said, "You will love this place.
At White Cottage Farm there's so much to do
and a big green pasture just for you!"

Around the farm there were cats and dogs,
birds and bugs, and a garden with frogs.
An empty pasture and hay in a heap.

But there were *nooooo* sheep!

"Oh dear!" said Grace. "There's no one like me. Just this woman, this man, and *their* family!"

"Are you their new baby?" the gray cat said. "You're wearing a diaper. They kiss your soft head."

"They call me their baby. But that's not what I am. My name is Grace. I'm a sheep. I'm a *laaamb*!"

Three pouncy kittens
bounced into view.

"Welcome home, Grace!
We've been waiting for you!"

"I can teach you to hop and race through the house."

"I'll even share my catnip mouse!"

"*Muck-mack, muck-mack!* I'm Mother Guinea."

"And we're her Guinea chicks! Welcome to our family. We'll teach you to do tricks."

"Can you stand on your head?"

"Can you walk on a rail?"

"Can you hide underneath the farmer's tin pail?"

"**Follow the leader**, Baby Grace. We'll show you all around this place."

They marched
through the barn,

past the farm's
white sign,

WHITE
COTTAGE
FARM

around the
greenhouse

and a full
clothesline.

They marched by the pasture,
so empty and green.

It was **the emptiest place**
Grace had ever seen.

Near a wood fence with a very big hole was a
cool, squishy place where two fat pigs rolled.

"Hello," squealed one. "How do you do?"

The other one grunted, "Glad to welcome you!"

"We're the potbellied pigs who live next door. You won't be lonely anymore 'cause we'll teach you to play and splash in the mud and snack on delicious dandelion buds!"

Baby Grace wailed, "There is no one like me—
just the mother and father and *their* family.
And an empty pasture and cats, chicks, and pigs.
And an old white house that's way too big!"

"*Baaa–baaaaa!*" Baby Grace said. She went to the barn and knelt by her bed. "Dear God, please send me a family. I need some sheep who are just like me!"

Grace knew God had heard her prayer, and so did another watching there. A big white dog patrolled the barn, and she knew all about the farm.

"Hello, my name is Winifred. I saw you kneeling by your bed. Baby Grace, please come with me. **There are some things you need to see.**"

"Each family is special,
whether large or small.

It's those who share your jokes and catch you when you fall. It's those who keep you safe and snug and give you warm and welcome hugs."

"It doesn't matter
who you are . . .

or who looks
just like you.

A family is **those you love** . . .

and all **those who love you!**"

When Grace looked into everyone's eyes, there was caring and warmth, and she realized, "I've got them, and they've got me. God gave me this family!"

She knew she belonged just where she was. And she felt very, *very* loved!

A few weeks later—what a surprise! Grace could hardly believe her eyes. The man brought two more little sheep home and into the pasture where they could roam. *"Baaa–baaaaa!"* the little sheep cried. "What is this place? It's so big and wide."

"**This is your home**," said Baby Grace. "And you are going to love this place. You don't know it now, but soon you will see . . .

"God brought *you* to our family!
We'll play and care for and love one another.

And no matter what—
we belong to each other."